I0520860

# Storylandia

## The Wapshott Journal of Fiction

### Issue 22

The Wapshott Press

Storylandia, Issue 22, The Wapshott Journal of Fiction, ISSN 1947-5349, ISBN 978-1-942007-13-5, is published at intervals by the Wapshott Press, now a 501(c)(3) nonprofit, PO Box 31513, Los Angeles, California, 90031-0513, telephone 323-201-7147. All correspondence can be sent to The Wapshott Press, PO Box 31513, LA CA 90031-0513. Visit our website at www.WapshottPress.org to learn more. This work is copyright © 2017 by Storylandia. The Wapshott Journal of Fiction, Los Angeles, California. Copyright © 2017 Philip E. Temples and is reprinted here with the copyright owner's permission.

Storylandia is always seeking quality original short stories, novelettes, and novellas. Please have a look at our submission guidelines at www.Storylandia.WapshottPress.org or email the editor at editor@wapshottpress.org

The Wapshott Press wishes to express our deepest gratitude to Michael C. Keith for his kindness and support of this issue of Storylandia. Mr. Keith's own writing can be found at his website at www.michaelckeith.com

Cover: "Outside a freak show at the Rutland Fair, Vermont, 1941," Library of Congress, (intermediary roll film) fsa 8c06780, www.bit.ly/2quheXF

# Storylandia

## The Wapshott Journal of Fiction

Founded in 2009

Issue 22, Summer 2017

Edited by Ginger Mayerson

## Table of Contents

# Albey Damned

By Phillip E. Temples

# Albey Damned

1

It was a hot, humid afternoon on the third day of August, in the year of our Lord 1934, and the good citizens of Denison, Oklahoma, had come to see the circus. They came that day, like on all days and in all towns, because they wanted a brief respite from life's everyday problems—finding food to put on the table for their family's next meal, holding the bank at bay just a little longer because they couldn't make last month's mortgage payment, or trying to coax the Model A to run just a while longer even though the carburetor was shot.

For some, the games and the rides lifted their spirits and those of their children's. It took them back to a happier era—to a time when they were truly carefree. Carefree, light, and happy in the sun. Yes, the circus held such a promise of respite from the harsh world! Willie wondered then, *why were these folks here in this dark corner of the universe, in my freak tent?*

Why did they come to gawk and stare at these *others,* who walked or crawled this earth with awkward gaits? Others, who possessed exaggerated features, or deformed arms and legs, whose bodies were stunted physically or whose genders were pathetically confused? Others, who exhibited grotesque and bizarre behaviors, who growled or barked or looked out with crossed-eyes, dripping drool from the sides of their mouths? Was it out of boredom or morbid curiosity? Perhaps. Was it an opportunity to feel fortunate or superior? To silently thank the Lord Almighty that He chose *others* and not *them* to bear these horrendous burdens? Possibly.

God made the freaks, of that Willie was certain. But it was his job to put them on display.

2

"Ladies and gentlemen, boys and girls! And now the moment you've all been waiting for! Without further ado! I give you! The horrific! The blasphemous! The one and the only! Devil Boyyy! Son of SAAA-tan!"

Willie made a sweeping gesture with his arm, parting the curtain with a flourish. The audience gasped in unison as Junior appeared. Junior parted his lips, bared his fangs, and hissed at the assembled crowd as he rattled the bars of his cage. Having witnessed these shows hundreds of times before, Willie was well aware that the sudden appearance of Junior was enough to make women and children swoon and grown men wet their pants. Up until that moment, however, a few of the Denisonians were beginning to grow restless after sitting through the acts proceeding Junior's—something that Willie and the other carnies didn't like to see in their business.

A fat, middle-aged woman in a flowery pink dress, sitting on the front row and sweating profusely, appeared to be in imminent danger of dozing off. A plump little wart of a girl sitting beside her—probably her daughter—was growing noticeably restless as she sat through the earlier shows, featuring Boris, the Mighty Miniscule Midget, Wanda, the Bearded He-Woman, and Frederick, the Elephant Man.

The little wart-girl wolfed down a corn dog on a stick, picking her nose all the while. Things got interesting, though, when her mother—the fat woman—woke up and saw Junior. She let out a blood-curdling scream that scared the bejesus out of poor Junior and practically everyone else in the tent. The little girl choked on her corn dog. She coughed and gasped for air. A man sitting behind reached out and slapped the girl hard between her shoulder blades. The girl expelled the piece of dog into her lap. She gasped loudly and knocked the undigested treat onto the ground in disgust. She then covered her teary-face with her chubby little arms and began to cry. The crowd murmured its approval for the man's heroic act. Willie was watching from stage left, behind the main curtain. He had to bite his arm to keep from howling with laughter. He knew that he shouldn't have reacted that way, but it was one of the funniest things he had seen in quite some time. It was a lot funnier than the acts they put on.

3

The story of the Albey Brothers Traveling Circus began back in 1909 when Robert "C.J." Albey, a former tavern owner from Toledo, Ohio, purchased the Boxer Traveling Circus. According to old C.J., he had been mesmerized as a young boy when the traveling circus came to his town: "I was always receiving whippin's from my old man when the circus stopped in Toledo because I would skip my chores and sneak off to see those daring young men on their flying trapezes, or huge elephants dressed in silver tassels standing on a single hind foot while balancing the other precariously over the scantily-clad women performers."

The years passed, and C.J. partnered with a childhood friend, purchasing a local pub house on the east side of town. Even as an adult however, C.J. maintained a special place in his heart for the traveling circus. Every summer, he'd ask his partner, Joe, "Can you hold down the fort for next couple of days? I'm goin' fishin." Joe, along with every other regular patron in the joint knew what that meant. The Big Top was in town.

As a bartender, C.J. would sometimes overhear customer conversation—on this particular occasion, the chatter of two patrons. They were both medical doctors schooled back east. After a few shots, one started to pontificate about the human condition— specifically, various human deformities put on display for their benefit during medical training: Siamese twins conjoined at the heads and hips; a man who was born without ears and a nose; "he-she" individuals possessing both pairs of sexual organs, along with a multitude of other poor souls with disfigurements.

When C.J. asked the physicians, what became of the specimens, he learned that some of the human oddities were locked up in relatives' basements for their entire lives. Those who were able-bodied were sometimes banished to the countryside to work as indentured farmhands. Others from the more well-to-do families were committed to sanitariums. Many of them, however, ended up in the carnival freak shows.

The subject fascinated C.J. He peppered the doctors with all manner of questions: "What kind of food do they eat?" "Do they get sick more easily?" "How long do they live?" "How would someone track these people down?" And so forth. He filed the answers away in the back of his mind.

Two years later, C.J. came across an advertisement in the *Cleveland Plain Dealer* announcing that the Boxer Traveling Circus based out of Omaha, Nebraska, was up for sale. Apparently, the business was down on its luck, its former manager having fled with the remaining cash to points unknown. The remnants of the outfit were marooned in a muddy field just outside of Stillwater, Oklahoma. After some considerable soul-searching, C.J. decided to sell his stake in the tavern to Joe. He telegraphed Boxer's company office, bought a train ticket to Omaha, and a week later, he bought the circus for a song. He left Toledo for good.

The circus came complete with two trucks, sixteen horse-drawn trailers, two donkeys, assorted farm animals, three broken-down rides, six big tents, two scrawny elephants, twenty-one workers, performers and two bonafide freaks.

C.J.'s vision for the new Albey Brothers Traveling Circus (there were no brothers—just C.J.) was to round up some of the best freaks in the country—after he fixed up the rides, of course. He placed advertisements, and procured the services of a number of free-lance *talent scouts* based in cities and towns back east, as well as in Chicago, Kansas City, Denver, and Omaha. These so-called scouts amounted to little more than two-bit con artists. But be that as it may, no one in the circus had ever thought to employ scouts before. It wasn't too long before old C.J. had a leg up on the competition. He was able to acquire some of the best freaks in the business.

4

Albey formally christened Junior "Devil Boy, Son of Satan" or "Devil Boy" for short. He was the undisputed star freak in the Albey Brothers Traveling Circus. In fact, he was one of the best freaks to grace the circuit in some time, according to many in the business. C.J. reckoned that the Enchanting Calloway Siamese twins couldn't hold a candle to Junior. Neither could Earl the Stupendous Snake Man or the Elephant Man With No Name.

It was surely true, thought Willie. After the opening shows in each new town, friends told neighbors who, in turn, told other neighbors about the frightening Son of Satan. His sinister reputation grew exponentially with each passing night. Willie put Junior in the cage draped with lots of chains, and even affixed a bible or two for good measure. It seemed rude and disrespectful to Willie to keep Junior locked up, and calling him by those ridiculous names.

"It's okay, Willie," Junior told him one day. "I don't blame you."

Still, Willie felt bad for Junior. He never called Junior by his stage name, except in the shows. Willie didn't refer to Junior as the "Devil Boy," even when he spoke privately with the other carnies. To Willie, he was always "Junior." Junior was more than just a good draw and an incredible freak. Junior was his friend.

5

When Willie was sixteen, he ran away and joined the traveling circus. Willie's Ma had died a year earlier; his daddy had little use for him. The old man would call Willie a worthless runt and beat him mercilessly for no reason. He'd belittle the child in front of people at every opportunity.

"Ain't no good fer nothin', that boy! Jest another hole to feed come dinnertime. 'Least I git me somethin' a use out of my hound dog."

After enduring countless beatings, Willie decided to run away from home. He soon found the means for his escape—the circus was coming to Millers Corner, just twenty-three miles as the crow flies from the farm.

Willie was bound and determined to do anything if they would only take him in—put up tents, sell tickets, shovel manure. Anything. Just so Willie could escape his miserable existence. Fortune was smiling on Willie that day when he came calling. The circus was short a hand, having lost a boy to desertion just two weeks earlier.

The first few weeks on the circuit, Willie began to wonder what he'd gotten himself into. The work was dirty and backbreaking and it was a lot harder than any of the farm chores he was used to doing. Worst of all, no one seemed to pay Willie any mind. Willie was miserable and exhausted. He barely had enough strength at day's end to drag himself to the supper table where he would eat alone. Luckily for Willie, after a few months, the foreman overheard him mimicking a barker one night while the boy was cleaning out the latrines. "I think you jes' might got a talent for barking, kid." The foreman told Willie he had a sincere-sounding, deep baritone voice, good modulation, and a slight nasal tint. Also, he'd seen Willie go out of his way to be friendly and helpful to the paying public. "You got a way with folks."

"All of these attributes, when combined," he said, "command the respect and admiration of the marks so as to entice 'em to dig deep into their pockets and part with their hard-earned pennies."

As far as Willie was concerned, barking sure beat the hell out of pounding stakes into the ground and shoveling shit.

6

"Hey, honey, come back here! I ain't got my money's worth yet!"

The drunken traveling salesman sat up in the bed and reached to grab Maxine's arm as she struggled to get up, but he was a second too late. "Hold on to your stick there, honey. I'm in need of a smoke and a pee. You just stay right there and rev it up and I'll be back in no time."

The man belched loudly. "Ho-kay. I'm a just a gonna ... wait right here for ya'... that's what I'll do..." He fell back heavily onto the mattress. The man was slurring his words badly; the prostitute was certain he would be fast asleep at any moment.

"Miserable, bad breath, limp dick son of a..." she muttered under her breath as she threw on some clothes to go outside to the outhouse. Maxine was also three sheets to the wind. But she managed to find the john's wallet in his pocket to see how much money he had on him.

"Fuck me," she whispered, noting the salesman was a full two dollars short of the agreed amount. "Fuck, fuck, fuck! Hell of a way to treat a lady." Maxine pocketed the bills and quietly shut the door behind her as she stumbled down the hallway to the backdoor.

After relieving her bladder, Maxine walked back to the porch and lit up a Lucky Strike. She took a deep drag to help sober up and to contemplate life.

Her's had been better. She'd arrived in town almost two years ago in the company of a good-looking man she'd met in St. Louis. Clyde was gainfully employed. He promised to show her the sights. It wasn't soon after, though, he broke that promise. Clyde had lit out of town with a younger, more attractive floozy. A friend said that they were headed for California. Maxine figured she'd never see him again.

She had held down a seamstress job for a while, but the pay was barely enough to cover the rent for her room in the flophouse. There was no money for food. Before she even realized it, Maxine had stooped to turning tricks. It wasn't something she was particularly proud of, but a girl's got to do what a girl's...

Suddenly Maxine was startled by a scraping noise coming from behind one of the trash cans nearby. "Who's there?" Maxine cried out. There was no reply.

"You better come out from behind that can, mister! I have a gun, and I know how to use it!"

She tried to calm herself. *It's only a raccoon. Or a possum.* She timidly approached the can, ready to curse and scream or do whatever was necessary to fend off an attacker.

Suddenly, she heard a faint whimpering. As she got closer, she could see a small figure crouching. *A little boy? Shaking in fear—in fear of me?*

"Darlin', are you okay? What are you doin' hiding back there?" In the glow of her Lucky Strike, Maxine suddenly caught a brief glimpse of the boy. What she saw terrified her—a wisp of a thing with practically no hair, and no nose to speak of. His ears were not round, but rather, pointed. And his skin! In this poor light, Maxine thought she was imagining things. But he looked... *An In'jun? An imp, a demon?*

Not long after Willie joined Albey Brothers, Junior was "recruited" from Leavenworth, Kansas, by one of the Albey talent scouts. Late one night, a drunken whore had found a half-naked, devilish-looking boy hiding behind a trash can. The sight of Junior scared her so badly that she went running to the Sheriff's office in spite of her inebriated condition. The Sheriff must have nearly locked *her* up after hearing the outlandish story she told of finding the son of Satan hiding in an alley off Broad Street. Something, however, must have compelled the Sheriff to go and check out her story.

When Junior was picked up, he was scared, ragged-dirty and half-starved; he wasn't talking sense. It was only later that the authorities made a startling discovery—Junior wasn't dumb or an imbecile. He spoke all right, but it wasn't English. Instead, it was a strange dialect that one of the Irish jail keepers said resembled Gaelic, but wasn't. Even so, the jailer couldn't understand a word of it. And to top it off, the boy punctuated the odd speech with assorted grunts and tongue clicks.

A few weeks after Junior took up residence in the county jail, word reached Frank Wilshire, one of the Albey scouts based out of Kansas City, Missouri, about a strange, freakish boy with almost no nose, pointed ears, reddish complexion, who was nearly hairless, and who possessed a frightening mouthful of chisel-sharp teeth—a boy who couldn't speak English or any other known language. This latter fact was important to Wilshire, since the boy wouldn't be able to explain to anyone where *home* was. It certainly would make his job easier.

Wilshire arrived two days later at the Sheriff's office brandishing a shiny twenty-dollar coin and a bottle of smooth Jack Daniel's to help initiate a dialogue. It didn't take much convincing by Wilshire for the Sheriff to quickly grant custody of the boy to the Albey representative. The Sheriff figured he was doing the boy (if you could call him that) a big favor by allowing him to be with his own kind. Besides, it wasn't safe for the child to remain in Leavenworth. A traveling preacher at a tent revival had nearly started a riot on the jail the night before, when he preached to the God-fearing townspeople that "the Sheriff was harboring the Devil's spawn" and that he should "hand over the varmint to the Army of the Lord forthwith."

7

The speed at which Junior learned to understand and speak English was nothing short of phenomenal. When he arrived, C.J. made Willie his ward and told him to talk to Junior and tutor him. Willie was like a big brother to Junior, who—if Willie had to guess—must have been 12 or 13 years old. Junior also received additional rearing in the living skills and social graces like, how to dress and bathe himself and how to shake hands and be polite—courtesy of Wanda, the Bearded He-Woman.

For months, Willie would spend nearly every waking moment when he wasn't working schooling Junior. At first, Willie simply pointed to trees, rocks, and trucks—naming them as he went along. "Horse," Willie would say, pointing at one of the horses. Junior would pause, appearing to ponder the word for a moment. He would obediently say "horse" back to

Willie, as best he could. Then, Junior would amaze him by attempting to use the word in an actual sentence. There was no doubt in Willie's mind that Junior was incredibly smart. Once he got used to Junior's physical appearance, Junior was a lot of fun to be with. The other carnies—with the exception of the freaks—never did take much of a liking to Junior.

Just a year after he came to the circus, Junior's knowledge of English was most impressive. His thirst for books was voracious. He devoured Wanda's and Willie's limited library collection. Junior especially liked non-fiction and history books. Willie found himself knocking frequently on C.J.'s door to borrow new titles.

"What do I look like, son—a public library?" C.J. would ask, throwing his hands up in mock disgust. He'd wave Willie inside, and then he'd point to his bookshelf while shaking his head. Despite his theatrics, Willie knew that C.J. was secretly pleased with Willie's visits to acquire more books, and with Junior's progress. Junior's knowledge of history and current events was impressive. Junior's spoken English was good, too, although he did speak with a strong lisp. Willie attributed the impediment to his cleft palette—or whatever you wanted to call it. There were other oddities about Junior, however, that had escaped the attention of management.

8

"That boy, Junior... he's so sweet," Wanda said to Willie one day.

The company was set up a few miles south of Little Rock, Arkansas, on a grassy knoll overlooking the town. It was gorgeous spring morning; the wild flowers were in full bloom. Monarch butterflies and jumping grasshoppers were everywhere, thick as thieves. Wanda and Willie were alone out behind the latrines.

"He has a heart of gold," she said. "But it isn't where it should be."

"What do you mean? *What* isn't where it should be?"

"You know... his heart." Wanda leaned over, and placed her hand on Willie's chest, over his heart. "Your heart is right here." She removed her hand, and then placed it near her left breast. "My heart is here, too. But, do you know where Junior's heart is?"

"No ma'am."

Willie swatted at a grasshopper that had ricocheted off the side of his head as he continued to listen, intrigued by Wanda's matters of the heart.

"I felt around him one day when I was dressin' him. It's right here." Wanda put her hand low on her hip, just above her right buttock.

"Thump-thump-thump. Thump-thump-thump." she continued. "Three of 'em! Three heart thumps, not two. Now, I can't rightly imagine *why* the good Lord would see fit to mess up his innards—not to mention his face and his private parts that way."

Wanda reflected on her own words for a moment as she tweaked her mustache. Then she sighed, while making a little kick with her left leg to dislodge a grasshopper that had crawled up her skirt. "I suppose we all have our crosses to bear."

9

Junior had no trouble fitting in with the other freaks: Wanda; Earl the Snake Man; Sally and Helen Calloway, the Siamese Twins; Boris the Midget; Samuel, the Human Grub; and The Elephant Man With No Name, who, in fact, did possess a name—Frederic. They all liked Junior's quiet, good-natured demeanor. And Junior was always pitching in, helping the others with their costumes or with rehearsing their skits, as well as reading aloud to the ones who didn't know how to read.

All of the freaks had their own ways of coping with the pain and boredom of carnival life. When Boris wasn't exercising, for example, he would be poring over picture books of the old country he was from— the Basques region, which straddled France and Spain. Boris performed hundreds of chin-ups daily, using a small metal rod braced across the door of his trailer. Willie would watch Boris do tons of push-ups, too— twenty or more push-ups at a time with his left hand, and then he'd switch to his right without breaking his rhythm. He possessed an incredible physique, even for someone who was only three feet, two inches tall.

A native of Philadelphia, Wanda liked to smoke Cuban cigars. She once told Willie that—much to her mother's consternation—her Uncle Harold introduced her to the joys of cigar smoking when she was only eleven years old. Wanda was very hairy as an adolescent and had resigned herself to the fact that she'd never attract a male suitor. Instead, she took up sports, excelling in men's sports like baseball and tennis. The only *feminine* sport that Wanda enjoyed playing was croquette. After her mother died, Wanda, then 19 years of age, packed up and headed west. She worked at a number of odd jobs along the way—a plumber's apprentice, a mechanic, but mostly in smoke shops and saloons. She tended bar and waited on tables. She'd often pull double-duty as the bouncer.

Upon observing her heavy-set, masculine features and hairy complexion most of the troublesome bar patrons—especially the intoxicated ones—were only to happy to cooperate and leave the premises, giving her little lip and wide berth in the process. Wanda tended to grow restless living in one place after just a few months, and one day the circus came calling her name. "I never looked back," she said. Wanda liked to thumb through Sears and Roebuck mail order catalogues and toss darts to pass the time.

Sally and Helen, the Calloway twins, were always preening themselves, doing up their hair and painting their nails. Conjoined at the hips and shoulders since birth, they shared similar physical attributes: curvy figures, with thick, jet-black hair, clear complexions and high cheekbones, pouting lips, and piercing green eyes. They were in their early thirties but they looked years younger. They were certainly attractive. It was not uncommon for wealthy circus-goers to slip a fine bottle of cognac or champagne to C.J. in exchange for the bragging rights of bedding the two sisters.

Sally and Helen were happy-go-lucky, giggly girls who were rarely sad. If one got down in the dumps, the other would make the other feel gay with a joke or a fond remembrance of a lover in a past town. The Calloway twins seemed to like Junior a lot. They'd ask Junior if he thought they looked pretty. Junior would invariably answer "yes" but then he'd turn red—a redder shade of complexion than his usual skin tone. Willie couldn't tell which of the twins had a crush on Junior. Perhaps both.

Samuel was nicknamed The Human Grub. Born with a stunted body, and no arms or legs, Sam grew up in a Catholic orphanage in Lexington, Kentucky. It had been his home until his thirteenth birthday.

It was at about that time when the new bishop of the diocese came to town and toured the orphanage. The bishop was appalled at this small aberration that, for so long, the nuns had diligently nursed and cared for. He reckoned that the home could only accommodate twenty-six children; it so-happened that Sam was the twenty-seventh. Sam might as well have been number *two hundred* and twenty-seven. The bishop discreetly contacted an Albey representative in St. Louis; arrangements were made to ship Samuel off to the circus. Sam arrived just three months later. He was the latest addition to their little group.

Samuel used a sort of crawling locomotion to get places. The carnies wrapped him up tightly in burlap bags. Wearing regular garb was out of the question since his crawling along the ground destroyed clothes in no time. The twins liked to dye his burlap bags bright colors: red, orange, and even turquoise. It made him easier to spot, too. Sam prided himself on being independent. He was able to move along the ground at a surprising rate of speed. He could even wiggle out of the bag and go to the bathroom by himself, if he had to. Once, Sam was nearly trampled to death by an elephant when their handler brought the elephants out for exercise just before dawn. It was a good thing that Sam possessed a healthy set of lungs. After that episode, Sam informed one of the crew when he was going to be out and about.

Samuel liked to be read to. And he especially liked to play checkers and tic-tac-toe, moving the checkers with his tongue, and making "Xs" and "Os" with a pencil gripped between his teeth. He was nearly unbeatable at both games. In all, Sam was a good-hearted kid.

Frederic had been cast away from his family

in Columbus, Ohio, at a very early age. Now in his mid-50s, he had survived far beyond the number of years the doctors had predicted. The circus was the only life that Frederic had ever known. The gross elephant-like abnormalities about his head, neck and arms extended to his extremities as well. His health was poor and his circulation was bad. After simple exertion, Frederick would get winded and his heart would race like a prairie dog's. He needed to spend a lot of time in bed simply resting. Frederick liked listening to stories that Wanda and Junior read to him. He especially enjoyed the Charlie Chan detective stories, in particular, "The House Without a Key" and "The Chinese Parrot." Junior and Wanda would take turns teaching him in reading, writing and arithmetic. Sometimes, Willie would get in on the act, too. Frederic held the books very close to his eyes, as the gross deformities that exaggerated his features and made him appear elephantine also affected his vision. Frederic was beginning to read some simple children's books all by himself. Junior seemed very pleased with Frederic's progress. He'd say to Frederic, "I was Willie's star pupil. And now, you're *my* star pupil."

10

One day, in between towns, C.J. declared a "Carney Day" where the rides and games were to be set up just for the carnies. It was typically great fun. Of course, the carnies all knew the various games— Skeeball, Whac-A-Mole, Darts, and Ring toss, among the others—were rigged. That was the fun part, trying to point out to the person operating the game when they had flipped a hidden switch or stepped on a foot pedal so as to make the game impossible for the mark to win.

Wanda also got into the act. Usually, the two Siamese twins—Helen and Sally—manned the Kissing booth. The fellows paid their pennies and lined up expecting two very sweet, passionate kisses on the lips. But sometimes, the curtain would part, and instead, Wanda would be revealed—sporting beard, mustache, along with her best smooching lips. It was explained to the men beforehand that this, too, was a game of chance and that they were obligated to claim their *prize*.

Even old C.J. got into the act. He reversed the rules on the "Shoot the Freak" game. He and some of the supervisors would dress up in hideous Halloween masks and don goggles and cardboard armor. They would taunt the *real* freaks to shoot at them while trying to dodge their soft rounds shot from low velocity air rifles.

Willie noticed that Junior was off in a corner. He refused to play the game.

"This is the only time you'll ever get the chance to shoot your boss and get away with it."

"I don't want to, Willie." The tears were beginning to well up in his eyes. "I... It brings up very bad memories for me. I think I was once hunted by men with guns."

11

One day, Johnny, who was a part of the ride crew, pulled Willie aside at suppertime. In a louder-than-necessary voice, and in front of many of the carnies, Johnny asked Willie if he preferred the company of freaks to normal people.

"What do you mean?" Willie asked.

"Well, you sit at the freak table at practically every meal! Now, I know you had to learn Devil Boy to talk when he first got here. But he's a big boy, now. You're always hanging around with him and his freak friends morning, noon and night. Say—you're not turning into a freak yourself now, are you?"

The rest of Johnny's crew: Eddie, Jeb, Jimmy, Tommy and Buford, were listening closely to the conversation. They started snickering when they heard Johnny's last comment. They were all having a good laugh at Willie's expense. Willie didn't like it one bit.

"They might be freaks," Willie retorted, "But do you know what? They're good company, which is more than I can say for you guys sometimes."

"Ouch! You hurt our *sensitive* feelings, Willie. Didn't he, guys?"

Willie was starting to get really angry. He was sorely tempted to reply *I'd rather spend my time with freaks than assholes any day* but he held his tongue. Willie turned his back on their laughter, and began walking away.

"Freak." Johnny pretended to disguise the word as a cough but there was no mistaking what he had said.

That tore it. Willie turned around and rushed back at Johnny. Johnny had already turned around to face his buddies following his last remark. Johnny never saw Willie charging him. Willie caught him square around the waist; he wrestled him to the ground. It took three of the guys to pull Willie off of Johnny—but not until Willie had landed a couple of good punches to his left cheek and jaw. Fortunately, word never reached management about the tussle.

Still, Willie wouldn't have regretted it, not even if they had docked him a month's pay. He did have to soak his hand in a bucket of ice for several hours.

12

One day, Junior and Willie were returning from chores when they happened to hear loud trumpeting coming from the elephant tent. Several crew were huddled near the entrance. The object of their attention was Penelope, the older of the two pachyderms owned by Albey Brothers. She was lying down on the ground, in obvious distress.

C.J. was there, too, as Junior and Willie drew closer to hear what they were saying.

"...could be impacted, boss," said Ernie, who did the doctoring for the animals and livestock.

"What are you fixin' to do?" asked C.J.

"Well, I don't rightly know. We're out of horse tranquilizer; ran out back in Nebraska. And without something to put her out, old Penny ain't gonna let me near her. I can't get a look inside her mouth, let alone pull it."

"Can't you just whack her up the side of the head?" asked Fess, who was one of the ride guys.

All heads turned in unison and shot Fess dirty looks. He got the message that it was a dumb idea.

Just then, Junior stepped forward.

"Mister Albey, sir? I think I can help."

Junior explained that he had a special rapport with Penelope. He would communicate to Penelope that she needed to cooperate and let the men examine her tooth and, if necessary, pull it.

"Gosh, I don't know, son. That's a lot of animal, there."

No doubt C.J. was thinking about the risk of losing his prize freak should Penelope—mad with pain—crush or maim Junior.

"Please, sir! I know this animal. I have... well, we've developed a *friendship*. I know she'll trust me."

Junior was very convincing.

C.J. looked at Ernie, who shrugged his shoulders as if to say, 'I don't have a better idea.'

"Okay, Junior. Now look, I don't want you taking any chances. If that elephant so much as *looks* at you the wrong way, I want you out of here. Ernie, have your rifle ready, just in case."

Fifteen minutes later, Junior was given the go-ahead. Only he, Ernie, and another man, Edgar, were allowed inside. Everyone else was ordered to keep out.

Junior walked over slowly and approached Penelope. Ernie stood by with a large pair of pliers. Fess stood at the entrance armed with a rifle.

The elephant initially was startled by Junior's approach. She swatted her trunk angrily to and fro, and tried to stand up.

"Shh... it's okay, Penny. It's just me. It's Junior."

Junior put his hand on the elephant's enormous head and stroked it gently. Penelope exhaled a huge breath and relaxed at his touch.

After a moment of gentle stroking, Junior reached over and lifted up one of her gigantic ears. He started to sing quietly into her ear. It sounded like a lullaby. Then, he started whispering to her in his native tongue that resembled Gaelic. A moment later, Penelope was out like a light, as if under a hypnotic spell. Ernie was amazed!

"It's okay. She's asleep now. You can open her mouth, and pull the tooth if you have to."

Ernie approached cautiously. He motioned Edgar to join him. Ernie handed Edgar the pliers, while he reached down and tentatively pulled open Penelope's mouth. After a few seconds of inspection, he grunted to himself and then he motioned to Edgar to hand him back the pliers.

Ernie glanced over to Junior.

"You sure about this, kid?"

"Yes, sir. She's asleep. She'll stay asleep until I wake her."

"Here goes."

Ernie held his breath, and grabbed onto the troublesome tooth and gave it a slight tug.

There was no reaction from the pachyderm.

Satisfied that she was unconscious; Ernie counted to three, and gave a mighty heave and yanked out the impacted tooth in one swift motion. Several of the men outside pumped their fists and voiced a congratulatory, but quiet, Huzzah. They were still afraid that any loud exclamation might awaken Penny.

Ernie backed away from Penelope, and motioned everyone to move out of the tent. When everyone was outside, Ernie took out a handkerchief and wiped his brow.

"I don't know how you did that, kid. That was absolutely amazing! What did you do... ah, what did you *say* to her?"

"I told her she was feeling very sleepy, and that she would sleep until I told her that it was time to wake up."

"You put that animal into a trance?"

"Yes. Shall I wake her now?"

Ernie didn't answer. He seemed not to fully comprehend what he had just heard. Ernie stared at Junior blankly. Junior waited patiently for an answer.

"Ah ... what did you say, kid?"

"I asked, 'shall I wake her now?'"

"No. No, I'll pack up the hole with a poultice first. Then we'll give her a few hours to rest, and for the swelling to go down."

Ernie walked away from the assembly, shaking his head and muttering to himself.

13

"Where do you come from?" Willie asked Junior, one night.

The light had long-since faded from the western sky as they sat alone next to a fire outside of the trailer that Junior shared with Frederic. The Missouri sky above was brilliantly lit with a million points of light. The Milky Way flowed in one long, unbroken band over their heads, across the heavens. Just then, a lone shooting star passed under the Little Dipper.

"I don't know, Willie," he replied. "I have only vague memories of my people."

Junior referred to them as "my people" instead of "my family." Willie wondered if Junior belonged to some pygmy tribe in Africa or South America. He recalled reading an article from *Life Magazine* once about a group of anthropologists who explored the wild jungles along the Amazon River. One day, the scientists stumbled across a secluded village that had never seen a white man before. The villagers spoke in a strange language that included screeching noises and tongue clicks. The scientists reported that the villagers shared everything—food, child-rearing, even wives. Perhaps Junior's people lived in one of those villages. It wasn't all that hard to imagine.

For a moment, Junior looked up into the sky longingly. Then he fixed his gaze back on Willie. The flickering flame from the fire cast an eerie illumination on his mouth full of spiked teeth.

"I only remember that someone kept me imprisoned, in total isolation. Before that, I think... I think I traveled a great distance." He added, "It's frustrating not being able to remember."

When he was bothered about something, Junior had the habit of clicking his tongue against the roof of his mouth, or rather, where there should have been a roof. Instead, in its place, there was only a thin strap of membrane. Willie thought of Junior's mouth as a kind of *echo chamber*.

Willie asked him how long he'd been alone and separated from his people.

"Many years, I think. My only recollection is of being locked in a basement or downstairs room of some kind. I remember hearing piano music playing above me until the very early hours of the morning. A woman would come to the top of the stairs and throw down scraps of food for me to eat. Every day or so, she'd place a bottle of alcohol on the top of the stairs. She was very afraid of me."

Willie poked the embers of the fire with a stick. A thousand little sparks leapt into the night heavens to meet their brothers and sisters.

"Did you have a ma and pa?"

"Yes. But I know that they are gone," he replied. "I don't know how I know this. I just do. I am convinced that they met some terrible fate."

Willie didn't share with Junior what he was really thinking when Junior told him of his suspicions. Perhaps Willie was too jaded from his experiences with the circus. Having worked with freaks for several years, and hearing all the stories from C.J. and the other carnies, he knew the more-likely truth: Junior's parents had abandoned him at an early age. It would have been romantic for Willie to believe that Junior had come from a race of rare, red pygmies, but he was a pragmatist at heart. Still, to share the other thought with Junior at that moment—that he had been abandoned—would have been especially cruel. Willie chose to remain silent.

Junior and Willie talked a little more about Junior's vague recollections of his people and his feelings that he had come a great distance. Willie asked him if he recalled having sailed across some vast ocean or ridden over the continent by rail car. He didn't. Later, Willie shared with Junior some stories about his upbringing. His mother who died of consumption. And his pa, who berated him and beat him constantly. Junior looked up at Willie with those big, sad eyes and those wicked sharp teeth. Then he reached out and put his hand on Willie's shoulder. "I'm so sorry for what you had to endure."

What he said amazed Willie. In fact, it moved him to tears. Willie thought of the pain and suffering Junior must have endured—for that matter, what Junior *would* endure for the remainder of his life. Yet Junior had this capacity to listen to Willie's petty, insignificant problems—problems that didn't hold a candle to Junior's—and express genuine sympathy. At that moment, Willie knew that he and Junior would be life-long friends.

14

The circus caravan was crossing the rich, fertile fields of the San Joaquin Valley in California on its way to

Sacramento. The troop set up camp overnight in an open field north of Bakersfield. C.J. was anxious to pick up the pace. They were a day behind schedule. One of the horses was exhausted; another was on the verge of becoming lame. Both the animals and the humans needed a few hours to rest.

Junior had to take a crap. They would be there for only a few hours, so there was no call for digging a latrine pit. Willie told Junior he'd grab a lantern and accompany him to a clump of trees a few hundred feet from the encampment.

"Willie, I appreciate it, but there's no need for you to bother."

"I'd feel better if you weren't out there alone, Junior. There are rattlesnakes in these parts. I nearly got bit myself last year. Better safe than sorry."

A sliver of a new moon was not all that bright, especially with the thick cloud cover, but Willie kept the lantern turned off as they made their way through the fragrant, knee-high grass to the tree line. The fireflies were in abundance. A hoot owl announced its presence nearby.

*Wha...?* Willie thought he heard something moving behind them, to their right. *There!* He could see two shadowy figures, approaching at a fast trot. Junior heard them, too. They both froze. Suddenly, someone clobbered Willie, and the lights went out.

Willie wasn't sure how long he had been unconscious. When he came to, his hands and feet were bound and his mouth gagged. His head was buzzing; something wet trickled down into his ear. He saw Junior. Junior was tied up and sitting on the ground against a nearby tree.

"The kid's awake," said one of the men.

Willie looked over and tried to make out the owner of the voice in the dim light. He didn't recognize the man. Off to Willie's left, however, was another man whom he did recognize—Jeb Barton. Barton was a carny, one of Johnny's crew. Willie never did care much for the guy, and he suspected the feeling was mutual.

Barton saw Willie staring at him. "What are you looking at, freak-lover?" he asked.

It was clear to Willie that these guys meant to do him and Junior greater harm. Willie's head hurt badly and his heart was galloping, but he tried to calm himself and focus on how they were going to get out of this dilemma. He struggled against the rope, but the men had tied him up pretty tight.

A third man, who was in charge—the others called him Luke—walked over and stood in front of Junior. Luke eyed Junior like he was a two-headed calf.

"Boys, that thing don't even look human! Guess that's why the doc wants him. I sure as hell will be glad when we get it delivered and get our money."

"What about the kid?" asked Jeb, referring to Willie. "He ain't no use to us. 'Sides, we got only one extra horse for the freak. Tom... Jeb, grab the shovels. Start diggin."

Willie was really starting to sweat now. He shuttered at the thought that his life might come to an abrupt end on this night; his neck slit, his body dumped in a shallow grave in a field in the middle of nowhere. Perhaps someone at camp remembered that he and Junior had come out here to take a shit. Maybe they'd hear the voices. He was hoping against hope that these guys would slip up and he would have a chance to fight his way out.

Willie looked over at Junior. He was gagged, but watching Willie intently. Willie felt his reassuring presence, and he knew what Junior was thinking at that moment, too: *Patience. Wait for an opportunity to make a move.* Willie believed they would make it out of this somehow.

As the two men continued digging Willie's grave, Junior sprang into action. Willie saw him briefly squirm. Somehow, he'd freed his hands. Then, with seemingly no effort, Junior reached down and broke the bonds on his legs. He then crept silently over behind Willie, grabbed the thick rope securing his wrists and, in one powerful yank, somehow snapped his bonds, too.

"Hey...!"

Luke spotted Junior's activities and let out a yell. He started towards the duo with a knife in his hand. Meanwhile the other two guys climbed out of the hole and began to head their way. Junior immediately leapt into the air onto Luke and sank his teeth into Luke's neck, ripping the man's jugular vein. Luke shrieked. He dropped his knife and tried to pull off his attacker. After a few seconds, Junior jumped off him and landed on the ground like an alert cat. Luke must have known he was mortally wounded. He wore a horrified expression, as he held both hands to his neck and spun in slow motion like a man in a death dance. He was no longer a threat. He was done for.

While this was happening, Willie quickly took off the gag, hobbled over to where Luke had dropped his knife and picked it up. It was drenched in Luke's blood. Willie cut the rope around his legs and then immediately assumed a fighting position. Jeb and the other man were facing Willie with their shovels in hand, ready to attack. Just then, a gunshot went off. Everyone froze.

Willie was never so glad in his life to see C.J. and his boss, Rob Fogerty, pointing their guns at the would-be assassins and ordering them to drop their shovels. After Willie assured them that he and Junior were both okay and that there were no other attackers, C.J. told him to take Junior and head back to camp.

"Get Wanda to look at your head. You might be need'n a couple of stitches."

"What are you going to do with Jeb and the other guy?" Willie asked C.J.

"Don't you worry about them, kid. You 'n Junior *get* now, you hear? We'll talk later."

The following morning, the crew was already on the road. Willie awoke in a strange bed with a severe headache. He was in Wanda's trailer. Wanda was waiting with a steaming hot mug of coffee. She told Willie he didn't need any sewing up, but she added, "You'll have one hell of a scar down your temple. That'll impress the ladies."

Later, Willie pestered Fogerty about what happened after he and Junior left. He told Willie that he and C.J. questioned the two at length. Their ringleader had recruited Jeb as their 'inside man' to help kidnap Junior. For the sum of 300 dollars the men were tasked with delivering Junior to the offices of a certain Doctor Ezeriah Whiting, M.D., out of Kansas City, Missouri. The two swore they didn't know what the good doctor wanted with Junior.

Willie shuttered to think what Whiting's intentions were.

"What did you do with them?" he asked. "You didn't just let them go, did you?"

"We administered some good old-fashioned

'carny justice,' kid."

"What?"

Fogerty frowned at Willie as if to say, 'Stop asking a bunch of fool questions.' He simply repeated himself.

"We administered carny justice."

He saw Willie's puzzled expression.

"Do I have to spell it out? You know that hole in the ground they was diggin' for you? Well, we made it a lot bigger. Now shut up with the questions."

15

Winter was Willie's favorite time of the year. It felt like the cycle was beginning again. The company would start its trek from California across Nevada, New Mexico, and swing through the Texas panhandle and head for the upper Midwest in late spring and early summer.

The circus was traveling a dirt road about a hundred miles west of Silver City, New Mexico, near the town of Cohito, en route to Las Cruces for a week's stay. Fogerty told Willie to go into town and pick up supplies. Junior begged Willie to allow him to come along. The last time Willie recalled Junior leaving camp was when C.J. told the foreman to take all the freaks into town to get doctored due to an outbreak of whooping cough in the company.

"Junior, if we get caught, there'll be H-E-Double-L to pay. And it won't be just me."

"I'll be careful, Willie. I just want to ride along. I won't be any trouble. I promise."

Willie dressed Junior in a big Mexican sombrero that Earl the Snake Man loaned to them to hide Junior's pointed ears, along with a brightly colored

Serape complete with orange and yellow fringes to cover the rest of him.

"You'll have to keep your mouth shut, Junior. I can't explain all of those teeth to the locals if you smile."

"You mean, like *this*?" Junior shot Willie a huge grin. Willie thought, *that grin would intimidate a shark, assuming the shark didn't roll over and drown first.* He reached over and gently punched Junior's arm. Junior did likewise, reaching out to Willie with his balled-up, four-fingered fist.

The trip into Cohito was uneventful, but the landscape was breathtaking. Twenty miles out of town, Willie slowed the truck to a crawl so that he and Junior could take it all in. They witnessed the splendor of a distant purple mountain range to the west. (Willie didn't know its name.) Saguaro cactuses were in bloom everywhere. Little desert rats scurried hither and yonder across the brush. Willie could even make out scorpions sunning themselves on the nearby rocks.

"It's so beautiful, Willie! Why doesn't *everyone* live here?"

"I guess people need jobs. They need to eat. Not much to do around here, except to admire nature."

"My home looked a little like this, I think," Junior said. There was a sad note in his voice. His eyes seemed focused on something far away.

The duo arrived in town. Willie parked the truck across the street from the general store. Armed with his shopping list, Willie instructed Junior to remain in the truck.

"Stay out of trouble," he told him. Willie should have known better. When Willie returned to the truck with the supplies fifteen minutes later, there was Junior, standing outside the truck and next to a horse that was tied to a hitching post, along with half the town. Junior told him later what had happened: the trough next to the hitching post was dry and the horse was thirsty, so Junior had gone to fetch a pail of water from a nearby well. Apparently, however, Junior's massive sombrero kept getting in his way as he bent over to fill the trough. So, he did a most logical and expedient thing—he took off the hat! Before long, the sight of Junior, with his pointy ears, pug nose and sharp teeth, standing next to a thirsty horse in the center of Cohito attracted all kinds of attention. In record time, the town square became a zoo. Actually, a circus. Along with one thirsty horse.

There were little kids gawking and a half-dozen or so Mexican women crossing themselves and fingering their rosary beads while mouthing prayers. All the while, patrons spilled out of the Savings and Loan and the general store across the street to see what the commotion was about.

Close to Junior stood an old priest. He was chanting something in Latin. The padre held a bible and a blind man's cane in one hand. With his other hand, he grasped a vial that had its cover removed. He was attempting to sling Holy water on Junior. The trouble is he kept missing Junior and hitting the horse in the head. The horse wanting no part of this holy equine sanctification ceremony grew more agitated by the moment. To top it all, two drunken cowboys sat on the sidewalk in front of the nearby saloon, thinking the whole affair was hilarious. They were hoopin' and hollerin' it up big time.

"It's okay, folks," Willie shouted, in his best barker's voice. "I'm with the Albey Brothers Traveling Circus." he babbled, quickly, "This fellow here—

he's not the devil. He's a part of our freak show. You needn't fear him. He's not going to hurt anyone."

Willie should have shut up then and there. But something caused him to utter one more unnecessary, asinine comment—a comment that he regretted the second it passed through his lips. He would have given real money to be able to take back. Willie would never forget the look of hurt and anger on Junior's face after he heard Willie say it.

"Leave him alone, now. This sad specimen here is simply a freak of nature. One of God's mistakes, I say! Nothing more."

Willie apologized repeatedly to Junior during the drive home for saying what he had said. But Junior wouldn't look at him during the whole trip. Not once. He remained silent the whole time. Willie couldn't blame him. He didn't particularly care much for himself right then, either.

16

It was always Rob Fogerty's idea when an idea worked, and someone else's when it didn't. Fogerty was the foreman, and Willie's immediate boss. His short, stocky frame and bright red mop of hair betrayed his heritage even before he opened his mouth and spoke in that thick Irish brogue. Fogerty was a lover and a fighter. The fights were generally the result of his numerous liaisons with the ladies (many previously spoken for, judging by the wedding rings on their fingers) along the routes they traveled. Fogerty's acts were practically legendary among the carnies. He had suffered numerous contusions and broken bones along with dozens of knife scars. "You should see the other guy," Fogerty was always fond of saying. It was rumored that Fogerty had fathered more red-haired bastards along the circus route than Carter had liver pills.

It was Fogerty's idea to add the burning bible trick to the show. Junior had grave misgivings about it, and Willie wasn't real keen on the idea either. Willie told Fogerty that they shouldn't do it. Fogerty responded, "You'll shut your yap and do it, if you know what's good for you."

Willie wasn't objecting on religious grounds. He just thought that the folks might overreact to it. Besides, a part of him didn't feel comfortable desecrating any holy scripture—whether it be the Bible, the Koran, or those Torah scrolls that the Jews read from.

Fogerty sent Willie to the apothecary in Kenning, Texas, to fetch a bunch of chemicals. The only chemical on the list Willie recognized was hydrochloric acid. He'd never heard of the rest. Fogerty had concocted this scheme where they would hollow out the inside of a bible, and place two vials of chemicals inside. Junior would approach the bible and pull a hidden string that would cause a firing mechanism to strike and break the vials inside allowing the liquids to mix. In a matter of seconds, the bible would start to smolder and eventually, burst into flames. Junior was told to make a "hissy fit" at the bible as though it were painful for him to touch the sacred object, or even go near it. Willie had modified his pitch based on what Fogerty told him to say. He also practiced some scripture reading.

Being a former barker, Fogerty should have known that this sort of thing could backfire on them. As it turned out, neither Fogerty nor Willie had *any* idea of the nightmare they were about to unleash.

"Folks, I have to ask for your indulgence just now," Willie began, slowly, warming up the crowd.

"We nearly had a tragedy of *unspeakable* proportions in the last town we visited. A little girl and her mother sat very close... *too close*, in fact... to the Devil Boy's cage. This little girl, God Bless her soul, reached up and tried to remove the Holy Scripture from the side of the monster's cage. As it turned out, both of them were scalded from the sputum from this monster!"

"Now, I can assure you... we have taken EVERY... SINGLE... PRECAUTION... known to God and man to keep you safe while we bring you this incredible spectacle.

"OBSERVE! Even though the cage is surrounded by multiple chains, forged from the strongest steel ever produced by the Bethlehem Steel Company of Bethlehem, Pennsylvania, you need to know this, my friends: the bible you see before you is the *real* shackle holding this unholy creature in check. It is an absolute NECESSITY!"

(Willie smacked his fist into the palm of his other hand.)

"Ladies and gentlemen, this physical manifestation of God's word... this very bible, here...

(Willie gestured over his shoulder)

"...has been blessed and sanctified in the name of the Father, the Son, and the Holy Spirit by the Bishop himself!"

(Willie made the sign of the cross.)

"If I was to...

(Willie paused and then he shuddered, visibly)

"...well, if I was to ever, EVER remove that bible

from the side of the cage, this Spawn of Satan, here, would tear through those chains just like they were cotton candy! And that *thing* would be on top of you with those sharp fangs... just... like... THAT!!"

(Willie snapped his fingers on the word *that* for dramatic effect.)

"Good people! I shudder to think of the depths of hell to which this varmint would drag your lifeless corpse if it ever escaped and returned back to its father. *So* deep into the bowels of Hades would he drag you that, I suspect, even with God's eternal love and salvation, your soul would never, EVER, gain entrance back into the Kingdom of Heaven."

Willie paused for a moment to wipe his brow.

"Now, I must ask...NO! I must INSIST that everyone who is now sitting in the front row... please vacate the row and find another seat farther back..."

That was Junior's signal to step forward towards the fake bible and trigger the chemicals. Willie had to hand it to Junior, given the humiliating circumstances that Junior was forced to work under, he was an excellent showman. Junior approached the bible just the way Fogerty had instructed him to do the night before. Timidly, cautiously, he reached out for the book as though his hand were approaching an open flame. A few in the audience took note of Junior's movements; they gasped and pointed when they saw him performing this unusual act. Undetected, Junior quickly pulled the trigger mechanism, and then he jumped back and bared his teeth and held onto his hand as though he had been burned.

"Look!" cried a young boy, as wisps of smoke began emerging seconds later from the Good Book.

"Everyone! Listen to me!" Willie pleaded. "Please remain calm! The scriptures of the Almighty protect us. He will not fail us."

Willie spoke very quickly now:

"The Lord our God which goeth before you, he shall fight for you, according to all that he did for you in Egypt before your eyes..."

Willie stopped quoting scripture for a moment, and looked over his shoulder. Still the book smoldered. He was waiting for the crescendo, to recite the final lines when the book would burst into flames—assuming it would. No one—not even Willie—knew how the marks in the audience would react to this bible-burning event, although Forgerty assured him several times that it would be okay and that old man C.J. had signed off on it.

Willie was beginning to get a very bad feeling.

"RUN FOR YOUR LIVES!!" shouted a man from the back row. He bolted out of the tent.

Then, all hell broke loose.

People were leaping and screaming and jumping and squalling and praying. One man began to roll on the ground and speak in tongues. He was stepped on by at least a half-dozen people darting to and fro.

"WILLIE...!"

Junior's voice was nearly drowned out by the noise of the ensuing pandemonium. Willie knew Junior was in no immediate danger; some months earlier they had installed a hidden door in the back of Junior's cage as a contingency. Willie saw Junior out of the corner of his eye grabbing the cage bars in the front. In the meantime, panicked people literally trampling one another to death. Willie saw a little girl in a blue dress go down; several grown men stepped on her head and torso numerous times. No one tried to pick her up off the ground. They seemed oblivious to the life they were snuffing out under their muddy boots.

Willie couldn't comprehend the nightmare that was happening around him. He froze. A horrible realization came to Willie: he—not Junior, not Fogerty, not C.J.—*he* was responsible for the mayhem and the injuries and the deaths. God was punishing him for his blasphemy.

The smell of peoples' fear was sickening. People careened into Willie; the contact was numbing. Willie looked at the cage and saw the bars were bent wide open. Junior was off to the left on the ground. He was trying to drag an old woman out from under foot by her leg. Willie wanted make it stop, to freeze time and fix it. But it just kept happening. There was so much noise.

Willie didn't remember how he came to be in a ball on the grass outside, lying in his own vomit. Willie flinched as a hand touched his shoulder. It was Junior's. He watched Junior's mouth move, and heard his voice coming through a fog. What was he saying? Willie had no idea.

18

After the disastrous show, the circus pulled up stakes and left Kenning in the dead of night. I heard later that old man Albey had had a very unpleasant conversation with the local constable immediately after the incident happened. C.J. handed the lawman five twenty-dollar pieces to show how sorry the entire circus felt about things and to help with the medical and burying expenses.

"Much obliged," said the constable as he

pocketed the coins, adding how he reckoned that it was all a horrible accident. He supposed that no one person was really to blame. "Not that barker-kid, or the kid's foreman, or even the freak" for the trampling deaths of the little girl, Sassy Horton, and Peter Washington, the old colored man who worked on a ranch outside of town. "Sometimes," he said, "these things are just acts of God."

The constable held out his hand again, indicating that *more consideration* would be required. C.J. scowled, but he complied, handing the man two more gold coins. The constable tipped his hat to C.J. and turned to leave C.J.'s office. But before he did, he added, "Now you listen to me, Carnival Man." His voice was cold.

"You keep tight wraps on that devil-freak of yours, and make damn sure this kind of thing doesn't happen again—especially that burning bible trick. Or we might be seein' one another again under less hospitable circumstances."

C.J. was so angry about the incident, especially having to endure a humiliating dressing-down from the local constabulary that he could hardly see straight. C.J. was especially incensed by Fogerty's explanation, "the kid was acting on his own, I had no idea what he was up to." C.J. was not born yesterday; he saw straight through Fogerty's lie. Forgerty received one hell of a verbal tongue-lashing. And he was docked an entire month's pay.

19

"It should come as no surprise to you that I'm really pissed off," C.J. told Willie the following day when he was called into C.J.'s office. Willie stood in front of

C.J.'s dark mahogany desk with ornate carvings along the front. C.J. had brought it with him from the old Boxer Circus offices when he took over the outfit long ago. A plush leather guest chair sat beside the desk, beckoning to Willie. But C.J. did not invite him to sit down.

"I know the kind of a bastard that Robbie can be sometimes." He paused for a moment to light his pipe, and then he sucked on it a couple of times to get it burning smoothly.

"Son, I've been told that you witnessed that little girl getting stomped to death. Is that correct?"

"Yes, sir."

"You seen it with your very own eyes, did you?"

"Yes, sir."

Willie's voice was cracking. He practically whispered the last response. Willie's head was hung low, and tears were welling in his eyes. Willie wasn't pretending to be sad and ashamed; he truly was. And the old man knew it, too. You couldn't pull one over on a carny, especially not old C.J.

"Well," he continued, "I was fully prepared to kick your ass from here to St. Louis after I heard what happened in your show. But, you know what? You've got a real *special* punishment reserved for you."

C.J. sucked in another puff from his pipe.

"Now, I *know* Fogerty told you to do it. I don't doubt that for one second. You're young and naive and you let your boss talk you into doing a damn foolish thing. I'm sure that he planned out every last detail, right down to the words you spoke, right?"

He continued, not waiting for a response—not wanting one, either.

"You needn't concern yourself with him. I'll deal with Robbie in my own way. But, *you!* You're getting a *different* kind of punishment. For the rest of your life, you're going to see those images in your mind. Every time you *lay me down to sleep* you're going to see the lifeless body of that poor little girl getting stepped on by grown men seized in a panic—a panic that *you* helped to create."

He paused for a moment to let the words sink in.

"Now, get out of here! Before I change my mind and start kicking your butt *anyway*."

## 20

Many months passed. Little by little, Willie began to put that awful day behind him and go on with his life. It was a Thursday afternoon just before dinnertime. Willie was basking in the bright, summer afternoon outside of Wanda's trailer along with Boris, Wanda, Frederic, Sam, the twins, and Junior. Wanda had borrowed a current copy of the *Kansas City Star* from C.J. for the troupe to read. It was just a week old.

"How many times have you beaten yourself?" Frederic asked Boris, who was playing solitaire.

"'Is not that simple. I sometimes cheat myself. You see?" He flipped a couple of the cards over to show them, and then he grinned. Willie didn't know what he meant as he wasn't a card player, but Wanda chuckled over what Boris had showed them.

Frederic, sporting his new reading spectacles, was sharing the comics with Sam. They especially enjoyed Buck Rogers and Tarzan of the Apes. Junior had the world news section. Willie was reading the regional section; it carried a story by A.B. MacDonald about a gruesome murder in Amarillo, Texas. Sally and Helen were painting their toenails a brilliant shade of red, while Wanda trimmed her beard with a scissors and comb.

Junior looked up, and asked, "Willie, have you been following the events in Europe?"

"Nah."

"This story talks about what's happening in Germany. It says that the Communists burned down the Reichstag building."

Willie looked up from his newspaper section; Junior saw the puzzled expression on his face. Junior explained.

"You know—the German Parliament building. The Communists burned it down. At least, that's what they claim. Chancellor Hitler is urging President Hindenburg to pass an emergency decree to ban the German Communist Party."

"That Hitler, he is evil man," Boris interjected. "He no like Communists, Gypsies, freaks—anyone who different."

"Hell, most of the people in this fucking carnival don't like us, Boris," said Wanda, who was looking away. She quickly added, "Junior, honey, you didn't hear that word, okay? Anyway, that don't make them evil. Assholes, maybe. But not evil."

Wanda turned and faced Willie.

"What do you think, honey?" She proudly showed off her handiwork.

"You missed a spot, right here." Willie playfully pointed one finger at his face, making a wide, sweeping gesture from ear-to-ear.

Sam started to giggle. He thought the joke was funny.

"Quiet, you little runt!"

Wanda reached over and pretended to smack Sam with the hand mirror. She brought the mirror up to her face to inspect her work one more time. Meanwhile, Sally was blowing on Helen's toes in order to dry the polish on her nails.

Willie turned to Junior and said, "Hitler's over there, and we're over here. I don't much care what they do in their own back yard, so long as they leave us the hell alone." Willie added, "The 'War to End All Wars'... right! I reckon it didn't quite live up to its reputation. I suspect they'll have another go at it. Sooner or later they'll get it right. What do you think, Junior?"

Junior said nothing in response. He frowned and clicked his tongue, and then he went back to reading the paper.

21

It was fall, and the company had begun its annual trek through the Great Divide, en route to winter stops in Nevada and California. It seemed hard for Willie to believe that he'd been with the Albey Brothers Traveling Circus for almost three years. These past few days, it seemed like everyone was a little on edge. Willie attributed it to the higher altitude of the Rockies. Frederic was certainly having more than his usual problems with shortness of breath.

Junior seemed to be especially irritable and restless. Willie had wondered what he had done to upset him. He asked Frederic about it one day after breakfast.

"It's not you, Willie."

Frederic wheezed as he drew breath.

"Junior's been a little withdrawn around everybody. Just yesterday, I asked him if everything was all right. At first, he didn't want to talk about it.

Then, he told me that he's been having vivid dreams. Not nightmares... *vivid dreams* he called them. He said he'd explain it to us soon enough."

Willie caught up with Junior later that night. As they stood outside of Junior and Frederic's trailer in pitch-blackness under the new moon sky, Willie told Junior about Frederic's comments about his dreams. He asked Junior, "What are they about?"

"Willie, if I told you, you wouldn't believe me. Or you'd just accuse me of making it all up. Or, worse—you would think that I was crazy."

"Ah, come on, Junior! This is *me* you're talkin' to. We've known each other a long time. I wouldn't think that."

Junior clicked his tongue a couple of times. He said nothing for a full minute. Then he sighed.

"Please do not repeat what I am about to tell you to anyone outside of our group, okay?"

"Scout's honor," Willie replied, crossing his heart.

"And especially not to Mister Albey."

"Double scout's honor. Now, come on. Out with it!"

"Okay," he began, quietly. "My dreams. They are of my people. I can see them. I can hear them, too. They're coming for me, Willie. They're communicating with me. They've found me, and they're coming to take me back!"

What he did and said next was nothing short of astonishing.

Junior reached up and pointed to a portion of the southern sky near Orion's belt.

"Up there, Willie. My home—it is up there."

Willie was dumbfounded. At first he didn't know what to say. He had half-expected Junior to tell him that he had been haunted in his dreams by angry mobs of Christian soldiers coming to lynch him, to send him back to Hades. God knows Willie had had that nightmare on more than one occasion. But this was... well, this was Buck Rogers stuff. This was the stuff of fantasy. Willie didn't know what to say.

"Junior, this is... extraordinary! You, ah... you say you can see them in your mind. What do they look like?"

"They look like me, Willie. Just like me!"

"And you hear their voices. Do they speak English, or the language you used to speak when you arrived here?"

"It really isn't a spoken language, Willie. It's more like their collective thoughts. They are logical, concise, and unambiguous. It all makes sense. And, I remember, now. I remember *everything*."

Junior proceeded to tell Willie the story about how he came to be in this backward, savage land known as America.

"My people and our entourage came to this world on a sort of combination cultural expedition-vacation. My... I guess you could call her my mother. She was an important politician. In your world, she would be the equivalent of a U.S. Senator—except, we have no countries. Our world is united under one government. Our vacation party arrived in the center of the United States, in the state of Kansas."

Junior stopped talking. He looked very sad. He seemed in no mood to continue the story.

"I'm sorry," Willie said. "I guess I can figure out what happened next."

"The others were attacked and killed," he said. "They were slaughtered."

"And you? You were the only survivor?"

Junior paused for a moment.

"In all of the confusion, I escaped. I lived off of the land for many months. I kept moving, constantly. Eventually, I made my way into a city. I'm not sure which one. The rest... well, you know about my imprisonment."

Willie stopped for a moment to catch his breath, realizing that he had been holding it for what seemed like eons. It was certainly one hell of a story. Willie didn't know whether to believe it or not. Had the circus life finally caught up with Junior and made him crazier than a bed bug? Or, was Junior telling the truth. He was, in fact, not a freak, but a being from another world? Willie knew him well enough to know that he wasn't spinning some yarn or tall tale. One thing was certain about Junior's story: *Junior* believed it.

"Junior, where are they? And how are you going to find them? You can't just go wandering off into the Colorado woods in search of a rocket ship."

"That won't be necessary. They know *exactly* where I am. And I know exactly where *they* are."

Junior pointed to a part of the heavens, in the eastern sky away from Orion's belt. Then he extended two of his fingers straight out.

"Do you see that bright star, just two finger-widths to the right of 'The Seven Sisters?'"

"Yeah, so?"

"Watch."

Willie watched the star for a few seconds. He thought that his eyes were playing tricks on him.

"What the—?!"

The *star* was moving—slowly, but deliberately—across the heavens, tracing a slow arc upwards. Willie knew enough about astronomy to know that the object was moving much too slowly to be a shooting star. And, the planets and stars didn't meander across the sky like that. It had to be their spaceship!

"It's them. IT'S THEM! ISN'T IT, JUNIOR?!"

Before Junior could answer, Willie reached over and grabbed Junior and lifted him off the ground, spun him around. Then he let out a whoop.

Willie was very happy for Junior. He was going home to his people. His wish had come true. He was finally going to belong.

22

Junior invited all the freaks could come with him. The following evening, they met in Wanda's trailer and talked about it. Every last person: Wanda, Earl, Frederic, Sally, Helen, Boris—even their newest arrival, Samuel—expressed their desire to embark upon this strange journey into the heavens with Junior, rather than stay behind and keep performing in the show.

Junior broke the news to Willie the next morning after breakfast. He couldn't blame them. Willie had a humorous thought, though—what if Sally had wanted to go, but Helen didn't?

"Willie. We voted. Everyone wants you to come, too." Willie was flabbergasted. He had always felt included by the group—but only up to a point. The fact that they would invite Willie to join them in this mysterious adventure felt like a great honor. He told Junior so.

"Junior, I appreciate it. I really do. But I'm not sure that I should go along. I'm just a redneck kid from Nebraska. Besides, you're going to need someone to help you escape and to run interference."

Junior begged him to reconsider. But Willie was only twenty-three years old, and he had hardly seen any of this world. Did he really want to go blasting off to another? Junior had explained to everyone the prospects of coming back any time soon were close to nil.

And, thought Willie, *what if I didn't fit in?* What if Junior's people were less forgiving than Junior? After all, Willie *was* the ringmaster of the daily show that put one of their own—the son of a very important person—on public display in a very humiliating manner. The others in their entourage were different. They had nothing to lose, and everything to gain.

Willie thought himself to be a coward. He was afraid of the prospect of leaving the Earth and rocketing off to some strange, faraway place. He was afraid of the unknown.

*Junior's friends are braver than I.*

23

They concocted a plan. The rendezvous point with Junior's people would be at a large clearing near Kingman's Pass, about ten miles up the road. Wanda would hot-wire one of the trucks and take off with everyone. At the same time, Willie would stay behind and disable the other vehicles and scatter the horses. Wanda recommended that he remove their distributor caps. Willie deferred to her, since Wanda's knowledge of automobile mechanics was more thorough than his. Frederic very wisely contributed a suggestion that the firearms in the storage locker mysteriously *disappear.* Everyone murmured his or her approval for this. Once the plan was put in motion, there would be no turning back. Without the freaks and the show, the carnival would suffer a disastrous setback. And, although Willie didn't mention it to anyone in the group, it was clear that he would be out of a job, and perhaps, even arrested for his complicity were they to discover it. Still, he was absolutely convinced that helping Junior and the others was the right thing to do.

24

In the final hours leading up to the escape, Willie was having serious second thoughts about his role in the whole plan. There was no doubt in his mind that Junior belonged with his own people. But to help deprive the carnival of its freak show was a death sentence for the troupe. It meant that a lot of good, hardworking people would be out of a job. Could he live with that on his conscience?

Willie sought the counsel of Sally Mae, the old, colored woman who was the camp cook. She had been with Albey's from the beginning. Sally Mae was a devout Christian and wise beyond her years. Willie had cried himself to sleep on Sally Mae's shoulder one night reliving the horrible tragedy resulting from the burning bible trick.

Without going into specific details, Willie told her that he felt obligated to help Junior achieve something at great risk and peril, which might also result in hardship for many others—including herself. Willie asked her what he should do.

The heavy-set woman smiled at him. She reached out and brushed his face with her ancient, calloused hands.

"Dat Junior! Ain't he a precious one? He *so* lucky to have you for a friend! If it was me, I'd sacrifice everythin' for dat boy. He dif'rnt. But I s'pose you already know dat."

What she said next shocked Willie. Sally Mae looked him straight in the eye and, with a mischievous smile, she pointed skyward.

"He from up *there*."

"How did *you* know Junior is from outer space?"

It was Sally Mae's turn to look surprised.

"Wha' ya talkin' 'bout, chil'? Junior ain't from outer space. He an angel! The Creator sent him to watch over us good folk here. And the animals, too."

## 25

That night, the crew executed their plan. At 3:00 AM Willie snuck out with Earl around to the back of the gun trailer. Using a crowbar, they broke the lock and each grabbed two-dozen assorted pistols and rifles along with several dozen boxes of ammunition. There was a creek that ran alongside the fairgrounds; they walked over to it with their burdens and heaved everything into the water. It wasn't very deep, so the guns could certainly be retrieved at daylight if they knew where to look.

"You get back with the others now, Earl. I'll take care of the trucks."

Willie shook his hand and wished him good luck. Then, he headed over to a circle of maple trees where the trucks were parked: the Bedford Six WLG two-and-a-half ton, two '27 Chevy Stakebeds and a '30 Ford one-and-a-half-ton pickup. It seemed a shame to mess them all up, but Junior's safety—and the safety of the others—rested in Willie's hands. He quietly raised the hoods and started to work.

It was now 3:35 AM. Willie stood by the makeshift corral with the horses. He had untied them all. Suddenly, Willie heard the remaining Bedford fire up, the result of Wanda's successful hot-wiring of the engine. That was Willie's signal.

"Yahhhh!! Yahhh!!"

Willie half-yelled, half-whispered, as he smacked at the horses' fannies and scattered them. They bolted in three different directions. A moment later, Willie heard someone rustling inside of the nearest tent. Old Ernie, who cared for the horses and the livestock, stumbled out in his long johns carrying a lantern. He stared at the stampeding horses in disbelief.

"I'll be a son-of-a..."

Just then, he turned and faced the tree that Willie was attempting to hide behind. For a split second before Willie ducked, the light from the lantern illuminated his face clearly. That was all the time it took.

"Who's that hiding there?"

A second later: "Is that you, Willie?"

It was too late. Willie had to think fast. He ran out from behind the tree.

"Ernie, there was three of 'em! I heard them when I woke up to take a piss. They broke into the gun trailer and then they made off with the horses!"

Ernie continued to stare at Willie for a moment.

"I don't think so, son. You're looking awful guilty hiding behind that tree there. Besides, you got all your clothes on. I don't think you been sleepin'. I think *you* was behind this."

"Don't be a fool, Ernie! Hey, you can believe whatever you want, but I counted at least three big, mean-lookin' guys sneaking around. They're probably after Junior." Willie continued, "Right now, we got to get those horses back. Why don't you go wake up Fogerty and the others and get some help?" Ernie didn't argue with Willie's logic. He looked at him as if to say, 'I'll deal with you later' and then he went off in the direction of Fogerty's trailer.

*How in the world did I think I could get away with this trickery? It's one thing to fool a mark, but it's quite another to pull the wool over a carny's eyes. And right now, I haven't pulled any wool over on Ernie's eyes despite the fact that he's rubbing sleep from them! I'm in deep shit. They'll grill me. If they learn about how I helped the freaks escape, they won't call in the Sheriff. They'll administer carny justice, instead. They'll roast me on a spit and then they'll hang me from a tree.*

Willie felt sheer panic. *I've got to get out of here!*

Suddenly, the prospect of rocketing off into outer space with Junior and the others didn't seem like such a bad idea to Willie.

It was now or never.

Willie reckoned that there wasn't enough time to restore the parts to any of the trucks. Fortunately, one of the mares hadn't wandered very far. She was still visible behind a clump of trees off to his right. Willie ran quickly over to where the mare was. When he got closer, however, the mare heard his approach and she started to get skittish. Willie stopped dead in his tracks, and then he calmly walked the last twenty or so paces so as to not spook the animal. Riding bareback was Willie's forte. He hoped like hell that he could ride swiftly enough to catch up with the others in time. Willie reached the mare; fortunately, she didn't bolt.

Now, jumping up on a horse without a saddle and riding her is pretty tricky stuff. They made it look easy in the picture shows. Fortunately for Willie, though, he used to do it all the time when he was back on the farm. His pa never let him ride, so he used to sneak out to the barn in the dead of night and without bothering to use a saddle, he'd hop awkwardly upon old Clayton and ride him around in the woods for an hour or so. It was very peaceful and pleasant, and it took the boy's mind off his problems. It was a nice escape from the drudgery and the beatings. Some nights, Willie had actually entertained thoughts about just going and going and never coming back.

Willie's thoughts quickly returned to the reality of the moment. This ride would be a horse of a different color. He would be riding for dear life. Willie mounted the mare and headed at fast gallop across the field, toward the main road. He could hear men shouting. Willie rode as fast as he could, holding on to the mare's long mane and squeezing his heels tightly against her sides.

Willie was really scared, now. It was official. He was an outlaw. If Junior and the group were gone by the time he arrived, it would be curtains for Willie. His mind began to run away with wild fantasies, like sitting in a rat-infested jail, half-starved, with open sores. Or sitting upon a horse under a broad chestnut tree, his hands tied behind him with a noose wrapped around his neck. He was waiting for the inevitable gunshot that would spook the horse followed by the gentle swinging to and fro as he gagged and coughed and sputtered, his life flashing before his eyes. Willie's final thought would be the image of the trampled little girl in the blue dress smiling up at him... her face smeared with blood and dirt.

Willie shuddered as he rode.

After a while, Willie's head filled with happier thoughts—thoughts of he and Junior. Like, the time he taught Junior how to first say 'horse' and 'apple'. Or the day Junior witnessed the elephant defecating and he said, "The elephant crapped big, Willie!" Willie also recalled the first children's book that Junior read unassisted. The smile on Junior's face was priceless.

Suddenly, Willie had a thought of Junior that he couldn't place from the past. It was a reassuring thought. It was as though Junior was saying to him, *don't worry Willie. You're okay. You're almost here. You'll make it!*

The thought was unlike any of the others. It almost felt as though Junior was actually inside his head. *Was it possible?*

As Willie rounded a bend in the road, he noticed an eerie glow above the treetops. The mare saw it, too. Willie sensed her slowing down. The animal and rider trotted up and around a clump of trees next to the road, and then...

Willie beheld something unbelievable. It had to be their spaceship. It was indescribable. Words could not begin to do justice to it. A blazing, white object was directly in front of them suspended roughly twenty feet off the ground. It was easily the size of a baseball field. One second it seemed rectangular, and the next it was spherical. And now it was diamond-shaped. It was so brilliant that Willie couldn't tell exactly from one second to the next what it was. It emitted an eerie, low-pitched tone. Also strange was the fact that with each shape transformation it seemed to dart around in jerky little motions—a few feet this way... then a foot that way. It never stayed in the same spot. Willie couldn't help but think that it was the most beautiful thing he'd ever seen in God's creation. Then he wondered if God even created it?

He caught a glimpse of Frederic and Wanda. Wanda was holding Samuel. They were standing next to Junior, directly underneath the object. Earl, Sally, Helen and Boris were nowhere in sight. Frederic looked over and saw Willie; he excitedly pointed him out to Junior. Just then, a brilliant flash of light shot out from underneath the spaceship. It enveloped Frederic. One second, he was standing there—the next, he was gone.

*Don't worry, Willie. That's how we get onboard. But hurry, they're coming!*

Just then, Willie shot a glance over his shoulder and saw what Junior was *thinking* to him: Johnny and Eddie, led by Rob Fogerty—all on horseback—were in hot pursuit. They were just a hundred yards away. They, too, however, slowed down when they observed the awesome sight of the spaceship—all except for Fogerty. He kept up his frantic gallop. Willie could see that he was holding a Smith and Wesson revolver in his hand. It was his private firearm that he kept with him in his trailer. Fogerty was aiming the gun straight at Willie. He clearly wanted to kill him.

Willie leapt off the mare and high-tailed it over to where the group was standing. A shot rang out. Willie felt something whizzing by his left ear.

"Run!" Willie cried. "He's got a gun! He's shooting at us!"

Just then, another brilliant curtain of light erupted from the ship, sideways, toward Fogerty. Willie looked over his shoulder at the pursuer, but then he started to laugh at the spectacle. Both Fogerty and his horse were up in the air, caught in the light. They were twisting and turning in slow motion, heads over heels (and hooves). The horse was whinnying and kicking his feet fiercely. It seemed that every time he kicked, man and horse would spin even faster. More beams leapt out, capturing the rest of the men and their horses.

*Wouldn't this make for an incredible carnival ride?*

Willie's thoughts were interrupted when another light beam shot down. It picked up both Wanda and Samuel. They were now gone.

*You're next, Willie,* Junior thought to Willie.

"Am I going in there?!" he shouted.

Willie glanced up at the prancing tetrahedral-sphere-cube above them, using both of his hands to shield his eyes from its brilliance.

*You're right. It would.*

*What?!* Willie thought back.

*The beam. It would make an excellent carnival ride.*

A bright flash of light hit Willie. He was enveloped in a warm, soothing sensation, followed by a feeling of weightlessness.

Fogerty's heart was pounding against his chest. He held on to his steed's neck for dear life. The horse seemed terrified as well. After a moment, men and beasts felt the tumbling sensation begin to cease. They all were gently lowered to the ground, unharmed. The brilliant light withdrew.

Forgerty's party heard a new sound now—a faint, high-pitched hum that emanated from the mystery ship. Then the brilliant object leapt into the heavens at an incredible speed. After only seconds had passed, it was nothing but a bright dot in the sky. Collectively, they stared at the dot for another minute.

One of the men muttered,

"Albey damned."

Phillip E. Temples has had over 120 works of short fiction published in print and online journals. A resident of Watertown, Massachusetts, Phil works as a computer systems administrator at a university. He is the author of the murder-mystery novel, "The Winship Affair" from Blue Mustang Press; a science fiction-fantasy anthology "Machine Feelings" and a paranormal-horror novel, "Helltown Chronicles," both from Big Table Publishing Company.

Thank you to the Wapshott Press sponsors, supporters, and Friends of the Wapshott Press.

Muna Deriane
Ann Siemens
Suzanne Siegel
Debbie Jones
Steven Acker
Jennifer Bentson
Kathleen Bonagofsky
Carol Colin
Ted Waltz
Cynthia Henderson
Aubrey Hicks
Nancy Lilly
Jeff Morawetz
Patricia Nerad
Amanda Nerad
Elaine Padilla
Bradley Rader
Laurel Sutton
Deana Swart
Kathleen M. Warner

The Wapshott Press is a 501(c)(3) not-for-profit enterprise publishing work by emerging and established authors and artists. We publish books that should be published. We are very grateful to the people who believe in our plans and goals, as well as our hopes and dreams. Our new website is at www.WapshottPress.org

www.ingramcontent.com/pod-product-compliance
Lightning Source LLC
Chambersburg PA
CBHW071210130626
46555CB00004B/1654